The Pages of Time

Art Vulcan

Published by Art Vulcan, 2024.

This is a work of fiction. Similarities to real people, places, or events are entirely coincidental.

THE PAGES OF TIME

First edition. October 22, 2024.

Copyright © 2024 Art Vulcan.

ISBN: 979-8227579133

Written by Art Vulcan.

Table of Contents

Chapter 1: 1
Chapter 2: 7
Chapter 3: 11
Chapter 4: 15
Chapter 5: 19
Chapter 6: 23
Chapter 8: 27
Chapter 9: 31
Chapter 10: 36
Chapter 11: 40
Chapter 12: 45
Chapter 13: 49
Chapter 14: 53

Chapter 1:

In a quiet corner of the library, Eleanor Marks sat, her nose buried in a book. The scent of old paper filled the air, a comforting aroma that never grew stale. Outside, the rain pattered against the window, creating a rhythmic white noise that complemented the silence of the room.

"Ellie," a voice called out, breaking the tranquil scene. She looked up to see Janet, her best friend and fellow librarian, peering over the bookshelf. "You have a visitor." Eleanor placed a bookmark between the pages and stepped out of the sanctuary of her favorite reading nook. At the library's entrance, a young boy in a rain-soaked coat was looking around curiously. His eyes lit up when he spotted her.

"Hi, Miss Marks," he said, droplets of water still clinging to his lashes. "I'm Timmy, from Mrs. Duncan's class. We're doing a scavenger hunt, and we need to find the oldest book in the library." Eleanor looked at the eager young face before her, the kind of curiosity that she hadn't seen in a child's eyes for a long time. She felt a spark of excitement, a rare occurrence in her predictable routine. "Welcome to Dunsford's Library, Timmy," she said with a smile. "Let's embark on this adventure together."

Guiding him through the maze of bookshelves, Eleanor explained the history of the library, her voice echoing in the vastness of the old building. "This library is a treasure trove," she said, "each book a gateway to a different world." Timmy's eyes grew wider with every step, his imagination no doubt racing as he listened to her tales of the books' origins. They arrived at the back, where the oldest tomes were kept, protected by a velvet rope and a layer of dust that had gathered over the years.

With a sense of reverence, she lifted the rope, allowing Timmy to enter the sacred area. The books here were bound in leather, their spines cracked and titles plates tarnished with age. "The oldest book here is 'The Chronicles of Dunsford,'" she told him, "It dates back to the 1600s, when the town was just a collection of cottages around the mill." Timmy's eyes sparkled with excitement as she carefully pulled out the heavy volume. "Be gentle," she warned, "These pages have seen centuries of life."

Together, they sat at an ancient wooden table, the book between them. Eleanor opened it to the title page, revealing ornate calligraphy and intricate illustrations. "It's like a treasure map!" Timmy exclaimed, his voice hushed with awe. She couldn't help but chuckle at his enthusiasm. "In a way, it is," she said, "It's a map of our town's past." As they turned the pages, she pointed out significant moments in Dunsford's history, bringing them to life with her vivid storytelling.

The library door creaked open, and a gust of cold wind brought in Mrs. Duncan and the rest of her class. Timmy's classmates gathered around the table, their faces reflecting the same wonder as their young guide's. Rain-speckled clothes and soggy shoes forgotten, they leaned in, eager to hear more. Eleanor felt a warmth spread through her chest, a feeling she hadn't experienced in a long time. It was the joy of sharing her passion with eager minds, of watching the spark of knowledge catch fire in their eyes.

THE PAGES OF TIME

"Everyone," she announced, "this is 'The Chronicles of Dunsford'. It's not just our town's story, it's a piece of us, of who we are and where we come from." The children nodded solemnly, sensing the gravity of the moment. Mrs. Duncan, a kind but firm woman, gave her a grateful smile. It wasn't often that someone could capture the attention of her rambunctious students so completely.

As Eleanor shared tales of the town's founding, of battles and romances, of triumphs and tragedies, the children were spellbound. They listened intently, their whispers of amazement and horror punctuating the air as she turned page after page. Timmy sat closest to her, his eyes never leaving the book, his small hands gently tracing the illustrations as if they could pull him into the very scenes they depicted.

The rain outside had turned into a storm, the wind howling through the cracks in the library's old windows, rattling the glass panes. Yet, inside, the atmosphere was one of warmth and wonder. The children were oblivious to the weather, fully immersed in the world unfolding before them. Even Janet had joined the group, her curiosity piqued by Timmy's excitement.

The pages grew thinner and more fragile as they approached the end of the book. "This is the oldest part," Eleanor said, her voice dropping to a whisper. "It tells of the very first days of Dunsford, when the land was wild and full of secrets." Timmy leaned closer, his heart racing with anticipation. The illustration on the final page was of a lone figure standing atop a hill, surrounded by a dense forest. The figure held a staff, a symbol of knowledge and wisdom. "This is the founder of Dunsford, Thomas Dunsforde," Eleanor continued, her finger tracing the outline of the ancient drawing.

The rain outside had turned into a storm, the wind howling through the cracks in the library's old windows, rattling the glass panes. Yet, inside, the atmosphere was one of warmth and wonder. The children were oblivious to the weather, fully immersed in the world unfolding before them. Even Janet had joined the group, her curiosity piqued by Timmy's excitement. As Eleanor closed "The Chronicles of Dunsford," the room grew quiet, the children's eyes wide with anticipation.

"But Miss Marks, what happens next?" Timmy asked, unable to contain their eagerness.

Eleanor looked up from the book, her eyes sparkling with the same excitement that had taken over Timmy. "Ah, young Timmy, it seems you've found yourself a new audience," she said, a gentle smile playing on her lips. She took a deep breath, her hands resting on the worn leather cover of the book. "Well, the next part of our story is quite the adventure," she began, opening the book to a page with a faded illustration of a castle under siege. "The town of Dunsford was once the site of a great castle, and it was during one such siege that our hero, Sir Henry, displayed his bravery."

The children leaned in closer, their eyes glued to the illustration as Eleanor described the battle in vivid detail. The clang of swords, the thunderous hooves of charging horses, the smell of the damp earth, and the feel of the cold, biting rain. She painted a picture with her words, and they could almost hear the cries of the soldiers and the whistle of the arrows as they flew through the air. Timmy's classmates were transfixed, their previous squabbles forgotten in the face of the epic tale unfolding before them.

"Sir Henry," Eleanor continued, her voice rising and falling with the intensity of the story, "was the youngest son of a poor knight. Despite his lowly status, he had a heart full of valor and a mind sharp as a blade. One fateful night, during the darkest hour of the siege, he had an idea that could change the course of the battle." She paused for a moment, allowing the anticipation to build. "He gathered a small group of loyal men and set out under the cover of darkness to sneak past the enemy lines. Their mission was to set fire to the enemy's supplies, which were stored in a cave just beyond the castle walls."

The children gasped collectively, and Janet couldn't help but feel a sense of pride for the town's ancient hero. "But it wasn't going to be easy," Eleanor said, leaning closer to her captivated listeners. "The cave was guarded by the fiercest of the enemy's knights, a man named Sir Blackthorn. His reputation was so fearsome that even the bravest of men trembled at the mere mention of his name."

Timmy's hand shot up into the air. "Miss Marks, what did Sir Henry do?"

Eleanor nodded, acknowledging his question. "Sir Henry knew that he and his men couldn't just charge in blindly. That would be suicide. So, they waited, studying the guards' movements from the shadows, looking for a moment of weakness." She paused, her eyes scanning the room as if searching for the enemy herself. "And when the moment came, they struck with the swiftness of a fox. Sir Henry led the charge, his sword glinting in the moonlight, and they fought their way into the cave."

The children's breaths held, their eyes wide with excitement. "What was inside, Miss Marks?" a girl in the back of the group whispered.

"Inside," she said, her voice dropping to a conspiratorial tone, "were not just the supplies, but also a secret chamber that held the enemy's most precious treasures, and a map detailing their next move. Sir Henry and his men had stumbled upon their enemy's greatest vulnerabilities."

With the storm outside growing more ferocious, the children's eyes reflected the flashes of lightning that illuminated the library. The story had become more than just words on a page; it was a shared experience, a journey through the annals of Dunsford's storied past. Timmy felt his heart pounding in his chest as he pictured the daring raid, the flames of victory licking at the dark sky.

Chapter 2:

Suddenly, the lights flickered. Thunder crashed outside, making the children jump. Mrs. Duncan cleared her throat, a gentle reminder of the time. "Alright, everyone," she said, "I think we've found our treasure. It's time to get back to school before the storm gets worse." With a collective sigh of reluctance, the children began to gather their things. Eleanor watched as Timmy and his classmates put on their wet coats and said their goodbyes. As they filed out, the warmth of their presence dissipated, leaving the library feeling eerier than it had before. The storm had intensified, and the wind's howling grew more persistent. Rain lashed against the windows, painting streaks across the panes.

Alone again, Eleanor felt a strange urge to explore further. The excitement of the day had stirred something in her, something that whispered of forgotten adventures and lost stories. She wandered through the library, her eyes scanning the rows of books. Her steps took her to the back, to a corner she hadn't visited in years. There, behind a dusty bookshelf, she noticed a discoloration in the wall. Pushing aside the heavy tomes, she found a small, unassuming door, hidden from view. It was made of the same dark wood as the shelves, with a tiny brass knob that gleamed faintly in the dim light.

Her heart racing, Eleanor turned the knob. The door creaked open, revealing a narrow staircase that spiraled downward into darkness. She paused, listening for any sound of the storm, but all she heard was the rhythmic drip of rainwater somewhere far above. With a deep breath, she stepped through the threshold, pulling the door shut behind her. The stairs groaned underfoot as she descended into the unknown, her hand sliding along the cool, damp stone wall for guidance.

At the bottom of the staircase, she found herself in a small chamber, the walls lined with more bookshelves. The room was dimly lit by a solitary candle flickering on a dusty table. The air was indeed thick with the scent of aging paper, and the mustiness tickled her nose. The books here were ancient, their leather covers cracked and spines bent with the weight of time. The room was a hidden sanctum, untouched by the modern world.

Eleanor felt as though she had stepped into a time capsule, each book a silent sentinel of the past. The shelves stretched up to a low ceiling, and she had to crouch to avoid bumping her head. She reached out tentatively, her fingertips grazing the spines of the ancient tomes. The room was a treasure trove of forgotten lore, a place where the whispers of long-dead authors filled the air with tales of yore. The candle's flame danced as she moved, casting eerie shadows on the book-covered walls. The musty scent grew stronger, and she realized that this place was not just old—it was ancient. The books were bound in materials she had only read about in history books, yet the pages looked almost new, untouched by time. Some had no titles or author, their origins shrouded in mystery.

Her eyes fell upon a particularly large tome in the center of the room. Its cover was made of a rich, dark leather, adorned with gold-foiled symbols that gleamed in the candlelight. It was bound with thick, leather straps that looked as though they hadn't been unbuckled in centuries. A shiver of excitement ran down her spine as she approached it. This book was different from the others—it pulsed with an energy she could feel in the air around her.

With trembling hands, Eleanor unbuckled the straps and opened it. The pages were thick, almost like parchment, and the ink was a deep, vibrant black that seemed to suck the light into it. As she began to read, she realized that the words were not written in any language she recognized. Yet, somehow, she understood them. They spoke of events that hadn't occurred, of people she had never met, of a world that was not of her time. The book was a living archive, a chronicle that spanned the entirety of the world's existence—past, present, and future.

The realization hit her like a bolt of lightning. She had stumbled upon something incredible, something that could change the fabric of the world's history. Her heart racing, she flipped through the pages, seeing snapshots of moments she had only read about, and others she had lived through as if they were happening right in front of her. Each turn revealed a new story, a new piece of the puzzle that was the library's hidden chamber. The books didn't just record the past, they chronicled the future as well, its pages filled with prophecies and events that had not yet come to pass.

Eleanor knew she couldn't read everything there and then. The sheer volume of information was overwhelming, and the thought of the books being forgotten in this dusty chamber was unbearable. She carefully selected one, a tome smaller than the rest, yet equally as mesmerizing. It was bound in a soft blue leather with silver embellishments. The pages whispered as she turned them, revealing tales of love and loss, of heroes and villains. This book contained the history of Dunsford up to the present day.

"Eleanor, are you okay?" Janet's voice called from the staircase, her footsteps echoing in the small space. "You've been down here for hours!" Eleanor looked up from the blue leather book, her eyes glazed over from the endless stories. "I'm fine, Janet," she called back, her voice strained. "I've...I've found something amazing."

Her friend's face appeared in the doorway, concern etched in her features. "What is it?" Janet stepped into the chamber, her eyes widening as she took in the sight of the ancient tomes. "These books... they're not just historical texts. They're records of everything. The past, the present, and the future." Janet looked skeptical, but the awe in Eleanor's voice was palpable. "I can't explain it, but I know it's true."

Chapter 3:

Eleanor held up the blue leather book. "This one, it tells the story of Dunsford, up until now." She flipped through the pages, showing Janet the detailed accounts of events they had both lived through. Janet's expression shifted from doubt to amazement as she recognized the descriptions of the town's recent history. "But it's what's to come that's truly incredible," she whispered. The candle cast shifting shadows on their faces as Janet reached out to touch the book. "What do you mean?" she breathed. Eleanor took a deep breath, her eyes shining with excitement. "This isn't just history, Janet. It's prophecy. Every book here is a piece of the world's fate, laid out before us." She paused, her gaze lingering on the gold-foiled symbols. "And we're part of it."

Janet stepped closer, her curiosity overshadowing any lingering doubt. "What does it say about us?" she asked. Eleanor's hand hovered over the pages, her heart racing as she searched for their names. Finally, she found it—a small entry, tucked between tales of town councils and harvests. "Here," she said, her voice quivering. "It speaks of us, of Dunsford's librarians, as guardians of these books." Janet's eyes grew wide. "We're mentioned?"

"Yes," Eleanor nodded solemnly. "And it says that when the time is right, we will be called upon to use this knowledge for the greater good." Janet's eyes grew as wide as saucers. "What does it mean?" Eleanor flipped through the book, her heart racing as she searched for more information. The pages grew denser with prophecy, each line hinting at monumental events that had yet to unfold. "It doesn't say much," she murmured, her eyes darting back and forth. "Just that we're to be ready when the time comes."

The storm outside had passed, leaving behind a damp chill that seeped into the hidden chamber. Janet shivered, wrapping her arms around herself. "We should go," she said. "It's getting late." With reluctance, Eleanor agreed. Carefully, she closed the book and placed it back on the shelf. As they climbed the stairs, her thoughts were racing. What did it all mean? What was she supposed to do with this incredible knowledge?

Once they were back in the main library, Eleanor couldn't shake off the feeling of excitement. She picked up the blue leather book and held it close to her chest. "I need to take this home," she told Janet. "I need to understand more." Janet's eyes searched hers, a silent question lingering in the air. "Okay," she said finally. "But promise me you'll be careful."

Eleanor nodded, the weight of her decision pressing down on her. As she left the library with the precious book tucked under her arm, she felt a strange mix of exhilaration and fear. The town of Dunsford held more secrets than she had ever imagined, and now she was a custodian of those secrets. The rain had stopped, leaving the cobblestone streets shiny and the air smelling of wet earth. She hurried home, eager to dive into the book's mysteries.

Once in the safety of her cozy apartment, she brewed a cup of tea and sat by the flickering fireplace. The blue leather book lay open in her lap, the flames casting an eerie glow on its ancient pages. As she read, she discovered that the book contained not only historical facts but also cryptic messages about the future. Each entry was written in a lyrical, almost poetic language that seemed to dance around the truth, hinting at events rather than stating them outright.

The hours slipped by as Eleanor devoured the book, her eyes scanning the words that seemed to pulse with a life of their own. It was as if the ink was a river, carrying her through the annals of time. She read of battles and births, of love and loss, and of a town that had seen more than its share of joy and sorrow. The book spoke of her ancestors, of their lives and the roles they played in shaping Dunsford into the place she knew.

As the clock chimed midnight, she stumbled upon an entry that made her heart stop. It was about her, written in the same cryptic verse as the rest of the book. "The keeper of tomes, in solitude she dwells, until the storm's fury calls forth the untold tales." It spoke of her discovery and the responsibility that now lay on her shoulders. The words were like a hand reaching out from the past, guiding her to what she was meant to do. "But what am I meant to do?" she whispered to the empty room, her eyes searching the page for an answer. The book remained silent, its secrets still veiled. Janet's voice echoed in her mind, a reminder to be careful. Yet, the thrill of the unknown was too great to resist.

Day after day, Eleanor found herself lost in the pages of the blue leather book. She read about events happening in real-time across the world, her heart racing with every turn. The book was a living chronicle, updating itself as history unfolded before her eyes. It spoke of wars and peace treaties, of discoveries and inventions, of love and betrayal. She watched as the ink danced and swirled, adding new entries and altering existing ones. The book was a window into the very fabric of reality, and she couldn't look away.

"Ellie," Janet called through the apartment door, "You've barely left your apartment in a week. Are you okay?" Eleanor looked up from the flickering pages, the room spinning slightly around her. "I'm fine," she called back, her voice muffled. "I'm just...researching." Janet's footsteps retreated, and she heard the door click shut. Alone again, Eleanor returned her gaze to the book. She had become obsessed with the real-time chronicles it contained. The book had become an addiction, a window to a world that she could not tear herself away from. Each night, she watched as the ink bled onto the pages, detailing events from every corner of the globe. It was both terrifying and exhilarating, a power she never knew existed.

Days turned into weeks, and the once-thin volume grew thick with the weight of new entries. Her eyes grew weary from the constant reading, and her mind buzzed with the cacophony of untold futures. Yet she couldn't stop. Janet grew increasingly concerned, her gentle knocks on the door met with muffled assurances that she was okay. But Eleanor knew she wasn't. She was changing, becoming something else—a guardian of secrets too great to comprehend.

Chapter 4:

One evening, as the last light of the setting sun painted her apartment in a warm glow, she found an entry that sent a cold shiver down her spine. "The storm clouds gather, whispers in the wind foretell of an ending," the book sang in its ancient verse. "The keeper must choose, the path of darkness or the light she must quell." Her eyes widened in horror as she read of a cataclysmic event that would befall the world. A choice she had to make, a decision that would shape the fate of millions.

Her hand trembled as she turned the page, the ink swirling before her eyes, rewriting the future as it went. The words grew clearer, the images more vivid. She saw destruction and chaos, a world torn apart by forces beyond human understanding. Then, as if the book sensed her fear, the page flipped back to a gentle scene of her quiet town, untouched by the impending doom. "The Keeper's hand guides the quill, the future is not set in stone," it whispered.

Eleanor took a deep breath and closed the book. Her mind racing, she tried to digest what she had just read. Each time she opened it, the future was different. How could she make a decision when the very fabric of time was fluid? Her thoughts swirled with the images she had seen, the potential futures that lay before her. Some nights, she saw a world of peace and prosperity, with Dunsford a beacon of knowledge and wisdom.

Other nights, she was met with scenes of destruction and despair, the town buried under the weight of unspeakable darkness.

As the days grew shorter and the nights grew colder, strange whispers began to filter through the town. The old oak tree in the square had bloomed out of season, and animals that had long disappeared from the region had been sighted in the nearby woods. The townsfolk spoke in hushed tones of unexplained events, of objects moving on their own and clocks ticking backward. Even Janet had mentioned a peculiar feeling that seemed to follow her, as though someone was playing with the very essence of reality.

Eleanor's heart pounded in her chest as the pieces of the puzzle began to fall into place. "The book," she murmured to herself, "someone's changing the past." News reports spoke of historical artifacts disappearing and reappearing, of battles that had never been fought and kings who had never reigned.

One rainy afternoon, Mrs. Jenkins, the town's oldest resident, hobbled into the library, her eyes wide with wonder. "Eleanor, dear," she said, her voice quaking with excitement, "have you heard? The statue of Thomas Dunsforde in the square—it's changed!" Eleanor felt the blood drain from her face as Janet looked at her, questioningly. "What do you mean, Mrs. Jenkins?"

"It's standing differently!" Mrs. Jenkins exclaimed. "The pose it's in now, it's as though he's pointing towards the east. It's been facing west for as long as I can remember." Janet leaned over the counter, "Could it have been vandals?" she suggested. Eleanor's eyes searched the blue leather book, her mind racing. "No," she murmured, "it's something more." She looked up, her gaze

THE PAGES OF TIME

distant. "I need to see it for myself." Janet nodded, her concern growing. "I'll come with you," she offered.

The two friends hurried through the rain, the square emerging from the mist like a mirage. The statue of Thomas Dunsforde indeed faced east, his staff pointing to the horizon where the sun would rise. Raindrops pattered against the stone, blending with the freshly etched lines that now marred the familiar features. "This can't be," Janet whispered, her hand flying to her mouth, "it doesn't make sense." Eleanor's eyes narrowed as she studied the altered pose. "The book," she said firmly, "Someone's changing history." Janet looked at her, bewildered. "What are you talking about?" Rain splattered against their umbrellas as the wind picked up.

"The blue leather book," Eleanor explained, her voice urgent. "It's not just a history book, it's a living record of our world. And someone's rewriting it." Janet looked from the statue to the book in Eleanor's hand, her eyes wide with disbelief. "But how is that possible?" Eleanor's eyes searched the horizon, her mind racing. "I don't know," she admitted. "But the changes are subtle. So far, only things that could be dismissed as errors or pranks. But if they keep altering the past, who knows what the future will hold?" The rain grew heavier, plastering their hair to their faces. "We need to get back," Janet said, her voice barely audible over the pattering rain. "You can't stay out here all night."

They rushed back to the library, the chill in the air seeping into their bones. Once inside, Eleanor placed the book on the counter, her hands shaking. "Someone's altering the past," she said, her eyes meeting Janet's. "But why? And how?" Janet looked at her, the color draining from her cheeks. "you really think that's what's happening?" Eleanor nodded gravely. "It's the only explanation that fits. And we have to find out who's doing this before it's too late." She flipped through the pages of the blue leather book, her eyes searching for any clue, any inconsistency that would point to the culprit. Each page held a universe of information, but it was the subtle changes that spoke the loudest.

"Look," she pointed at an entry that detailed a recent town event. Janet leaned in, squinting at the faintly altered ink. The original description of a joyous summer festival had been overwritten with a somber account of a rainstorm that had never occurred. "This isn't right," Janet murmured. "But who could do something like this?"

Eleanor's gaze fell on a name that was etched in the book's margins, a name that didn't belong in the annals of Dunsford's history—Aetheria. "We have to go back," she said, her voice low. "To the hidden chamber." Janet nodded, her eyes reflecting the gravity of the situation. They made their way through the library, the candles flickering as they passed. The chamber felt colder, the air heavier with secrets unspoken.

Chapter 5:

In the dim candlelight, Eleanor searched the shelves for the gold-foiled book, her eyes scanning the spines. "It's here," she murmured, pulling it out and placing it on the table. Janet leaned over her shoulder as she carefully turned the pages, her eyes widening as she saw the unfamiliar name woven through the prophecies. "Aetheria," she whispered, the name foreign and yet resonating with a strange familiarity. "Who is she?"

"I don't know," Eleanor replied, her eyes still scanning the ancient text. "But she didn't exist before." Janet leaned in closer, her eyes widening as she saw the name etched into the margins of the gold-foiled book. "How is that possible?" she whispered, her voice echoing in the chamber. "These books are not just records," Eleanor said, her voice trembling. "They're a living archive of our world, and someone is writing themselves into our history." Janet looked at her, her face a mask of shock. "Why would someone do that?" Eleanor's eyes searched the gold-foiled pages. "I don't know," she said, her voice tight with urgency. "But we have to find out. If they're changing history, it could have disastrous consequences."

The candle on the table flickered, casting eerie shadows across the room as the two friends pored over the book. The pages grew denser, the entries more frequent. "Look," Janet pointed to a section that spoke of a great battle, the ink still fresh and wet. "It's like they're rewriting it as it happens." Eleanor nodded, her eyes narrowed in concentration. "We need to find a pattern, something that links these changes." They studied the texts late into the night, their eyes growing heavy yet they didn't find any sort of order or pattern in the new additions.

In a moment of sheer frustration, Eleanor slammed her hand against the bookshelf, causing the ancient tomes to rumble and shift. Suddenly, a book fell to the floor with a thud, its pages fluttering open. As they stared at the book, figures began to emerge from the pages, stepping out into the candlelit chamber as if from a painting come to life. First was Sir Bertrand, clad in gleaming armor, his eyes wide with astonishment. "Where am I?" he boomed in a medieval accent, his dramatic flourish at odds with the quiet library.

Next, Pippa, a nimble thief in a tattered cloak and a wry smile, slipped out of the pages of a different book. "Well, I'll be a pickled herring," she exclaimed, looking around the room. "This isn't the tavern I was expecting." She winked at Eleanor, her eyes sparkling with mischief. "Madame," Sir Bertrand bowed deeply to Pippa, "you do not belong in this realm of dust and ink." Pippa's grin widened. "And you, sir, don't belong anywhere without your trusty steed."

The third figure to emerge was Ernest, a detective from the pages of a noir novel. He adjusted his fedora, taking in the surroundings with a world-weary gaze. "This is no ordinary library," he murmured, eyeing the gold-foiled book on the table. "What's the deal, doll?" he asked Eleanor, his voice gruff yet curious. "What in the name of Shakespeare's left sock is going on here?" Eleanor and Janet stared at the three literary figures before them, stunned into silence.

"It seems we've been...summoned," Sir Bertrand said, his voice booming in the confined space. "But for what purpose, pray tell?" He looked at Eleanor expectantly, his hand on the hilt of his sword. Pippa sauntered over to them, her eyes gleaming with excitement. "I say, this is better than any tavern tale I've ever heard. Tell us, lass, what's the adventure afoot?" Eleanor swallowed hard, trying to reconcile the reality before her with the one she had known just moments ago. The characters from the books looked as perplexed as she felt, each glancing around the library as if searching for an exit back to their own pages. "I'm sorry," she began, "I didn't mean to pull you out of your...stories." Sir Bertrand looked at her, his face a mix of confusion and chivalry. "Fear not, fair lady," he said, his voice echoing in the small room. "We shall aid thee in thy quest."

Pippa leaned against the bookshelf, her hands on her hips. "Let's get down to brass tacks," she said. "What's the trouble in your world?" Janet looked at her friend, her eyes wide with disbelief. "Someone's altering history," she said, her voice shaking. "We need to stop them before it's too late." Pippa's smile grew sly. "Altered history, you say? That's more my alley than fighting dragons." She winked at Eleanor, who felt a glimmer of hope. Maybe, just maybe, these unlikely companions could help her navigate this new, uncharted territory.

Ernest lit a cigarette, the smoke curling up towards the cobweb-covered ceiling. "So, you're telling me," he began, his voice gruff and skeptical, "that someone's playing puppet master with the past, and we're the marionettes." He took a drag, his eyes narrowing as he studied Eleanor and Janet. "What makes you think we're the ones to stop 'em?"

Eleanor looked at the detective, her heart racing. "I don't know," she admitted. "But the book..." she gestured to the gold-foiled tome on the table, "it's been altered. And it's affecting our world. We need your help to figure out who's behind it." Pippa sauntered closer, her eyes alight with curiosity. "And what's in it for us?" she asked, a glint of mischief in her gaze. "Do we get a slice of this reality pie?"

Sir Bertrand's hand went to his heart. "For valor and honor, we shall assist thee," he declared, his chest puffing out. "But beware, for the one who doth meddle with the threads of time is a foe most cunning." Pippa rolled her eyes. "And probably has no sense of humor." Eleanor managed a small smile, "Thank you," she said. "We'll figure out what's happening together."

Ernest took a step closer, his eyes scanning the room. "Look, I don't know much about this 'timey-wimey' stuff," he said, flicking the ash from his cigarette into an empty teacup. "But I do know that whoever's behind this is playing a dangerous game. We need to get to the bottom of it, fast." Janet nodded in agreement, her eyes wide with excitement. "But how?" she asked. "How do we stop them?"

Pippa picked up the blue leather book and flipped through its pages. "Well, let's start with the source of the trouble," she said, her eyes sparkling with mischief. "This little tome seems to be the heart of the problem." She leaned in, her nose almost touching the page. "It's like it's alive," she murmured. "The ink moves like a river, changing the story as we speak." Sir Bertrand unsheathed his sword with a dramatic flourish. "Then we must guard it with our lives!" he exclaimed. "For if the flow of time is corrupted, we may all be lost to the annals of forgotten lore!"

Chapter 6:

Eleanor couldn't help but feel a little overwhelmed by the sudden influx of characters from her favorite genres standing before her. "Guys, please," she said, her voice a little shaky. "We need to stay calm and figure this out." She took a deep breath, trying to compose herself. "We need to find out who's rewriting history and why. And we need to do it without anyone else finding out."

"Fear not, milady," Sir Bertrand said, his eyes shining with valor. "For I, Sir Bertrand the honorable, shall fight beside thee in this quest for truth and justice!" Pippa snickered. "Sounds like you've been hitting the mead a bit too hard, old man," she said, nudging him with her elbow. "But I'm with you. This is more exciting than swiping a silver spoon from the Duke's kitchen."

"And I," Ernest spoke up, his voice gruff but firm, "will use my detective skills to unravel this mess." He took a long drag on his cigarette, the smoke curling around his words. "But we need to keep it low-profile. The last thing we want is the local five-o getting their hands on this book." Eleanor nodded in agreement, her eyes scanning the trio before her. "Okay, let's get to work. We need to find any clues, any anomalies in the library that could lead us to the person who's been altering the past." Janet nodded eagerly, her eyes lighting up at the prospect of a real-life mystery to solve.

"I shall be your eyes and ears in the annals of time," Sir Bertrand declared, his armor clanking as he moved closer to the table. "If there be a scent of foul play, I shall sniff it out!" Pippa rolled her eyes. "Keep it down, will ya?" she whispered, glancing around the library. "We don't want to alert the culprit." Ernest studied the book, his brow furrowed. "Looks like someone's been playing fast and loose with the plot," he murmured, flipping through the pages. "But why would they do it?" Janet leaned over his shoulder, her curiosity piqued. "Maybe it's for power," she suggested, "or to change something in their own life."

Pippa's nimble fingers danced along the spines of the books, searching for any clue that might be hidden in plain sight. "Or for a good laugh," she said with a shrug. "Some folks get their kicks messing with heads, especially if they can do it from the shadows." Eleanor's eyes searched the gold-foiled book, her heart racing as she found the first clue—a delicate, almost invisible signature in the corner of one page. "Look at this," she whispered, pointing to the name that seemed to shimmer in the candlelight. "The Time Keeper." Janet squinted. "What does that mean?"

"It means," Sir Bertrand spoke with gravity, "that we face an adversary of great power and cunning. One who wields the quill that shapes the very fabric of existence." His gaze fell upon the blue leather book, now lying open to reveal a page swirling with a tempest of ink. "The Time Keeper," Pippa murmured, her eyes narrowing. "I've heard whispers of such a person in the shadows of our tales. They say he—or she—moves through the pages unseen, leaving chaos in their wake." Janet leaned over the table, her eyes widening as she took in the significance of the name. "We have to find them before they change something that can't be undone."

THE PAGES OF TIME

They searched the hidden chamber, their eyes scanning the dusty shelves for any sign of the elusive Time Keeper. The air grew thick with the scent of aged parchment and the whispers of forgotten secrets. Janet found an ancient scroll tucked away in a corner, its edges yellowed with age. "Look at this," she said, her voice hushed. "It's a map of the library, but it's not like any map I've ever seen before." The parchment was covered in cryptic symbols and lines that twisted and turned in impossible ways. "It's like a labyrinth," Eleanor murmured, her eyes tracing the pathways. "But to what end?"

Sir Bertrand stepped forward, his sword at the ready. "Perhaps it's a clue, a puzzle to be solved," he suggested. "The Time Keeper could be leaving us a trail." Pippa rolled her eyes. "Or it could be a trap," she said, her voice laced with skepticism. "But if it's a map, then it's gotta lead somewhere." She took the scroll from Janet and spread it out on the table, her nimble fingers tracing the intricate patterns. "It's definitely not your run-of-the-mill treasure map," she said, her eyes narrowing. "This is more like a blueprint for reality itself."

Eleanor studied the scroll, her mind racing with the implications. "We need to understand this," she murmured, her heart racing. "The Time Keeper's power is growing, and we can't let them change our world any further." Janet nodded, her eyes glued to the swirling lines. "But where do we start?" Sir Bertrand stepped closer, his eyes scanning the intricate patterns. "The map seems to indicate a hidden chamber," he said, his voice low. "Perhaps within the very heart of the library." Pippa's gaze darted around the room, her mind clearly racing. "Or it could be a metaphorical heart," she said. "A place of power or significance."

"We must tread carefully," Ernest warned. "The Time Keeper is not likely to leave their secrets out in the open." Janet nodded, her eyes gleaming with determination. "But we can't ignore this. If they're rewriting history, who knows what they'll change next?" The five of them scoured the chamber, their eyes peeled for any sign of the elusive figure. The air was thick with the scent of dust and ancient knowledge as they sifted through scrolls and tomes. Janet's hand brushed against a book that seemed to pulse with a strange energy. "Here," she whispered, pulling out a tome bound in leather that was eerily similar to the blue book. "Look."

The book was titled "Chronicles of the Invisible Hand," and its pages were filled with cryptic entries about those who had tried to change the course of time—and the consequences that had followed. "The Time Keeper seeks power," Eleanor murmured, her eyes skimming the pages. "But what is their ultimate goal?" Pippa snickered. "Probably to be the star of their own story," she said, her voice light. "This is no laughing matter," Sir Bertrand said, his face stern. "To meddle with history is to invite chaos and ruin." Eleanor nodded solemnly. "We must act swiftly, but with caution. We know not the extent of their power."

"But how do we find someone who can move through time like a ghost?" Janet's voice trembled with fear and excitement. "We follow the breadcrumbs they've left," Ernest suggested, tapping the map with a knowing smile. "Look for patterns, clues in the books they've touched." They all turned to the blue leather book, its pages shimmering with the echoes of recent changes. "This book," Eleanor said, her voice low, "it's their lifeline. If we can track the alterations, we might be able to predict their next move."

Chapter 8:

Sir Bertrand leaned over the table, his gaze intense. "The map speaks of a nexus," he said, pointing at a symbol in the center of the scroll. "A place where the threads of time converge. If we can find it, we may be able to confront this Time Keeper." Pippa squinted at the symbol. "It looks like the library's stained glass window," she mused. "Could that be the key?" Eleanor's heart skipped a beat. "The window," she breathed. "It's a representation of the town's history. It's the most significant place in the library." Janet's eyes widened with understanding. "We have to check it out," she said, already moving towards the hidden chamber's exit. The others followed quickly, their footsteps echoing through the library as they made their way to the main hall.

The stained glass window dominated the room, casting a kaleidoscope of colors across the wooden floorboards. The figures in the glass looked out over the town's evolution, from its founding to the modern day. "It's beautiful," Pippa said, her voice filled with awe. "But where's the nexus?" Eleanor approached the window, her eyes scanning the intricate patterns. "The map mentioned a symbol, something that would stand out." Ernest, the detective stepped closer, his gaze sharp. "Could it be one of these figures?" He pointed to a glass representation of Thomas Dunsforde, the founder of the town. Janet nodded. "Or maybe it's not a symbol we can see."

"Look," Sir Bertrand interrupted, his finger tapping a spot in the corner of the window, "this is not of the same craft as the rest." A small, almost imperceptible flaw in the glass glinted in the candlelight. "It's a trapdoor!" He exclaimed, his voice bouncing off the high ceilings. They stepped back, staring in amazement as a section of the wall swung open, revealing a hidden staircase. The stale air of the chamber was replaced by a cool draft, hinting at a long-forgotten space.

"We must proceed with caution," Eleanor warned, her heart racing. "The Time Keeper could be anywhere." Janet nodded, clutching her book tightly. "We can't let them catch us off guard." The three literary characters looked at each other, their expressions a mix of excitement and nerves. "Ladies first," Sir Bertrand said, gesturing to the staircase with a flourish. Pippa rolled her eyes. "Thanks, gallant," she quipped, and with a swiftness that defied her corporeal state, she darted through the hidden doorway. The stairs creaked under her weight, leading them into darkness. Janet followed, her flashlight casting an eerie glow on the ancient stones. "It's like we're in a dungeon," she whispered. "Or a crypt," Eleanor added, her voice barely above a murmur.

Sir Bertrand brought up the rear, his sword at the ready. "Whatever the case," he said, his voice echoing in the narrow space, "we shall not be daunted!" They descended into the bowels of the library, the air growing colder with each step. The stairs opened up into a chamber lined with dusty bookshelves, their contents seemingly untouched by time. The blue glow from the gold-foiled book grew stronger, guiding them deeper into the labyrinth of forgotten lore. "The Time Keeper's scent is thick here," Pippa murmured, her nose to the air. "But their motives are as elusive as a shadow on a moonless night."

Eleanor paused, her hand on a book titled "Chronicles of the Forgotten." "Maybe they're seeking redemption," she offered, her voice filled with hope. "Someone who wants to right a wrong from their own past." Janet nodded, her eyes scanning the shelves. "Or power," she said. "To change the course of history, to be remembered forever." The detective, ever the pragmatist, spoke up. "Or maybe it's greed," he said, his voice gruff. "The desire to control the very fabric of reality."

Sir Bertrand raised his sword. "Whatever their motives, we must find this Time Keeper," he declared. "To track such a being, we must look for inconsistencies, ripples in the fabric of our world." Pippa snickered. "Or just a bunch of messed up prophecies," she said, her eyes gleaming with mischief. "But how do we find someone who can skip through time like a stone on a pond?" Janet asked, her voice filled with doubt.

They moved through the library's catacombs, the air thick with the scent of decaying pages. The gold-foiled book grew heavier in Eleanor's hand, its power palpable as the paradoxes grew more frequent. Suddenly, the town's bell tolled in the distance, its sound echoing through the corridors. But it wasn't the familiar chime of the hour. It was a pattern, a code. The books around them quivered as if in response. "The fabric of time is unraveling," Janet murmured, her eyes wide with fear. "We need to move faster."

"Aye," Pippa agreed, her hand resting on the hilt of her dagger, "before we all become forgotten footnotes in someone else's story." They hurried down the corridor, the sound of the erratic bell tolls growing more urgent. Suddenly, the world around them lurched. A bookshelf shuddered, its contents spilling out onto the floor. "What was that?" Janet's voice was tight with fear. "A paradox," Eleanor murmured, her eyes wide. "The Time Keeper's meddling is getting out of hand." The town's clock tower, a landmark that had stood proudly for centuries, vanished into thin air outside the library's stained glass window. The townsfolk, their memories altered, walked by without noticing. "This is getting serious," Eleanor said, her voice shaking. "We have to find the Time Keeper before it's too late."

"Indeed," Sir Bertrand agreed, his armor clanking as he hurried to keep up. "We must tread with the grace of a gazelle and the cunning of a fox." Pippa grinned. "Or the sneakiness of a pickpocket," she quipped, darting down an aisle. They followed her, the sound of their footsteps muffled by the dusty carpets. "We're getting closer," Janet whispered, her eyes glued to the blue leather book. Its pages fluttered, revealing snippets of altered events.

Chapter 9:

A portrait on the wall changed before their very eyes, the subject's expression morphing from one of pride to despair. "It's like reality itself is a manuscript," Pippa mused, her eyes wide with wonder. "And someone's scribbling in the margins." They turned a corner to find a townsperson dressed in medieval garb, completely out of place in the modern library. The man looked around, bewildered, before fading away like a mirage. "This is getting out of hand," Janet murmured, her eyes filling with worry. "We can't let this go on."

Eleanor's mind reeled as she stumbled upon a memory of her mother's face, both smiling and tear-stained at once. "It's...it's changing me," she whispered, her voice trembling. "The Time Keeper is not just rewriting history, but our very essence." Janet took her hand, her grip firm and reassuring. "We're almost there," she said. "We can't let them win." The blue book grew warm in her grasp, its pages fluttering faster than ever.

The group gathered around a dusty book titled "The Case of the Vanishing Clockmaker." The book's cover depicted a shadowy figure in a top hat, a timepiece clutched in its grip. "This is where it starts," Eleanor murmured, her eyes locked onto the book. "We need to go in." The literary figures exchanged glances, their expressions a mix of determination and trepidation. "If we go in," Pippa said, "there's no telling what we'll find."

Sir Bertrand stepped forward, his hand on the book. "We shall not be swayed by fear," he declared. "For the sake of Dunsford, we march onward!" With a collective nod, they opened the book. A swirl of ink and paper engulfed them, transporting them into the foggy streets of Victorian London. The cobblestone pathways were slick with rain, and the distant sound of a foghorn echoed through the mist. Gas lamps flickered, casting an eerie glow that painted the world in shades of amber and black.

"THIS ISN'T JUST A BOOK anymore," Janet whispered, her eyes wide. "It's like we're living it." The detective looked around, his eyes sharp. "We need to find the clockmaker," he said. "That's where the Time Keeper's tampering began." They moved through the alleyways, the blue leather book guiding them with a soft glow. The fog grew thicker, the shadows dancing on the damp walls like living creatures.

Pippa stopped abruptly, her hand to her head. "The memories," she gasped. "They're fighting each other, trying to take hold." Sir Bertrand looked at her with concern. "What do you mean?" he asked, his sword at the ready. "It's like I'm remembering two different pasts," she said, her eyes scanning the foggy street. "One where I was a lady of the manor, and another where I was a thief on the streets."

Eleanor nodded, her brow furrowed. "The Time Keeper's alterations are affecting us all," she murmured. "But we can't let it distract us." She clutched the blue leather book tightly. "We need to find the clockmaker." The group moved through the fog, the cobblestone streets slippery underfoot. The air was thick with

THE PAGES OF TIME

the scent of coal and wet wool, and the distant toll of a bell chimed out of sync with their steps. They approached a shadowy alley, the blue light from the book growing stronger.

As they turned the corner, a cloaked figure emerged from the mist, hunched over a makeshift desk, quill in hand. The figure looked up, revealing a pair of piercing eyes that seemed to see through them. "You've found me," the Time Keeper said, their voice a low purr. "But I'm afraid you're too late." The figure flicked their wrist, and the alleyway shifted around them, the buildings morphing and twisting like the pages of a book caught in a tornado.

Sir Bertrand charged forward, his sword gleaming in the flickering gaslight. "You shall not escape us, foul trickster!" he bellowed. The Time Keeper chuckled, their hand darting to a nearby book. The street scene around them rippled, and suddenly they were in a bustling medieval market. The smell of roasting meats and the sound of haggling replaced the foggy London alley. "You're not the first to challenge me," the Time Keeper said, their voice echoing through the stalls. "And you won't be the last."

Pippa, her nimble feet quick to adapt to the new setting, slipped through the throngs of people, darting around the Time Keeper. "Why are you doing this?" she called out, her eyes searching for an opening. "Why change what's already written?" The Time Keeper's eyes gleamed. "Because it's fun," they said with a malicious smile. "To see the rats in their maze scurry when the walls shift."

"We won't let you do this," Eleanor said firmly, her voice cutting through the cacophony of the market. She stepped closer, the blue book in hand, the pages fluttering with agitation.

"You're playing with people's lives!" The Time Keeper's smile grew wider, revealing a set of teeth that seemed too sharp to be human. "But what is life without a bit of drama?" They gestured to the book. "You've all played your parts so well, but it's time for a twist in the tale."

"We demand answers!" Janet's voice was as sharp as the blade of Sir Bertrand's sword. "What do you want with the world's history?" The Time Keeper's eyes danced with amusement. "Oh, the same as anyone who craves power," they said. "To bend it to my will. To make the narrative mine." Their hand hovered over the open book, the quill poised to strike. "But fear not, for the show is just beginning." Earnest stepped forward, his detective instincts kicking in. "What's your game?" he growled.

The Time Keeper's smile grew cold. "Game? This is no game, dear detective," they said, their eyes flicking to the gold-foiled book in Janet's hand. "This is the essence of existence. And I am its conductor." Before they could react, the figure flicked their wrist, sending a ripple through the pages. The market scene around them shifted again, the stalls morphing into the grandeur of an ancient Roman amphitheater. The air grew heavy with the scent of sand and sweat.

"Your interference ends now," the Time Keeper declared, their form flickering like a candle in the wind. Sir Bertrand's eyes narrowed, and he lunged again, his sword slicing through the air where the figure had just been. The Time Keeper reappeared at the top of the amphitheater's steps, their laughter echoing through the stone arches. "You're no match for me, mere creations," they taunted, the quill in their hand leaving a trail of shimmering ink in their wake.

"We're not just characters in your story," Pippa spat, her dagger drawn. She dashed through the crowd, using her knowledge of shadows and distraction to cut off the Time Keeper's escape. The crowd around them grew more and more confused, their memories colliding as the very fabric of the scene changed. The Time Keeper's eyes narrowed. "Perhaps not," they admitted. "But this is my stage, and I write the script."

Chapter 10:

The Time Keeper flipped through the pages of a giant book that had appeared before them, the pages fluttering with a life of their own. "You're changing things," Eleanor said, her voice shaking. "But why?" The figure looked up, the blue glow from the book highlighting their grin. "Because I can," they said simply. "Because the thrill of it all—it's intoxicating." Janet stepped forward, her eyes blazing. "You have no right to do this!" she exclaimed.

"Ah, but I do," the Time Keeper said, their voice dripping with malice. "You see, I am the narrator of the cosmos. The scribe of fate. And I tire of the same old storylines." They leaned in, their eyes gleaming with madness. "I crave the thrill of the unexpected, the joy of chaos." With a flick of their wrist, the scene around them shifted again, the Roman amphitheater crumbling into the background as they were transported to a futuristic cityscape. Neon lights danced across the sky, and the sound of hovering vehicles filled the air.

"You're mad!" Janet exclaimed, her grip tightening on the blue book. The Time Keeper laughed, a chilling sound that seemed to resonate through the very air. "Mad? Perhaps. But also a master of my craft. Now, if you'll excuse me, I have a universe to rearrange." They disappeared into the bustling crowd, leaving the four of them standing dumbfounded in the alien environment.

THE PAGES OF TIME 37

"WE CAN'T LET THEM GET away!" Sir Bertrand called, his sword still at the ready. Pippa nodded, her eyes scanning the futuristic landscape for any sign of the elusive figure. "They're playing a dangerous game," Eleanor murmured. "And we're the pawns." Janet took a deep breath, her mind racing. "We need to find a way to track them," she said firmly. "The book!" Earnest exclaimed, pointing to the gold-foiled book in Janet's hand. "The prophecies! Maybe there's something in there that can lead us to their ultimate plan."

The five of them huddled around the book, their eyes scanning the pages for any clue. The blue glow grew brighter, pulsing with the rhythm of the futuristic city. "Look here," Janet said, her finger pointing to a line of text that hadn't been there before. "It says, 'When the guardian's light wanes, seek the heart of the library's maze.'" The detective's eyes narrowed. "The heart of the maze," he repeated. "Could that be the nexus we're looking for?"

Sir Bertrand nodded. "We must return to the library," he said, urgency in his voice. "The fabric of our reality is fraying." They stepped back into the swirling ink, the world around them bending and stretching like a Salvador Dali painting. The library's hidden chamber materialized, the stained glass window now a jagged shard of light in the wall. The books around them looked diseased, pages peeling away like leaves on an autumn tree.

Eleanor's eyes fell upon the shelf where the gold-foiled book had been. A cold dread filled her heart as she saw the empty space. "No," she whispered. "The Time Keeper has it." Janet's eyes searched the room, her brow furrowed. "And they're escalating," she said. "Look at the books." They turned to see pages fluttering away like butterflies, leaving gaping holes where once there had been words. Entire histories were being erased, forgotten.

"The future's unraveling," Pippa murmured, her hand to her mouth. "Look at the dates on the pages. It's happening faster than we thought." The books grew thinner, the pages fewer, as if being erased by an invisible hand. "The Industrial Revolution," Janet breathed, her eyes wide. "It's gone." The once-proud spines of tomes detailing the era's triumphs and tragedies had become as bare as the day they were bound. "No more engines, no more progress," she whispered, as saw the outside world change through the stained glass window.

The town outside was now a patchwork of eras, the library's window showing a landscape where horses pulled carriages alongside silent, unused assembly lines, their steel skeletons rusting in the sun. The pyramids of Egypt had vanished from the desert, leaving only a memory of their grandeur in the minds of the confused scholars who had studied them. The townsfolk outside stumbled about, their lives a tapestry of forgotten moments and altered realities. "They're rewriting everything," Janet murmured, her eyes wide with horror. "The Industrial Revolution, the Renaissance, even the Roman Empire!" Sir Bertrand's hand tightened on the hilt of his sword. "This cannot stand," he said, his voice low and fierce. "We must stop them before all is lost." Pippa nodded, her own eyes blazing with determination. "We know where they're heading," she said. "The nexus."

"But why?" Eleanor's voice was small, lost in the cacophony of the dissolving library. "What could drive someone to such madness?" Janet looked at her, her expression grim. "Power," she said. "The desire to control destiny." But Eleanor was shaking her head. "No," she said slowly. "It's more than that." The gold-foiled book grew heavier in her hand, its pages fluttering with the weight of untold futures. "The Time Keeper," she murmured, her eyes scanning the shelves, "was once like us. A scholar, seeking truth." Janet raised an eyebrow. "How can you be so sure?" she asked. Eleanor met her gaze, her eyes shining with the light of realization. "Look around us," she said, gesturing to the decaying books. "Their power comes from the very essence of our world's history.

They crave the knowledge that we seek in these pages, but they've lost their way. They've forgotten that knowledge is a gift, not a weapon." Sir Bertrand and Pippa exchanged looks, the gravity of her words sinking in. "What are you suggesting?" Pippa asked, her dagger at the ready. "We must understand them," Eleanor said firmly. "Find the reason behind their obsession." Janet's eyes searched hers. "And what if there is no reason?" she asked. "What if they're just a force of chaos?"

Eleanor took a deep breath, the scent of ancient leather and dust filling her lungs. "Then we fight for order," she said. "But first, we need to find the nexus. The heart of the library's maze." They moved through the library, the pages of reality peeling away around them like the layers of an onion. The books grew fewer, the shelves barer, until they reached a grand chamber at the center of the labyrinth. A single pedestal stood in the middle, a gleaming crystal pulsating with a blue light.

Chapter 11:

"The Heart of Chronos," Janet murmured, her eyes wide with awe and fear. "This is where the Time Keeper is drawing their power." The crystal's light grew brighter, casting an eerie glow over the ancient tomes that still stood, clinging to existence by a thread. "We must be careful," Eleanor said. "If we disrupt their power source, we could cause a paradox that could destroy everything." But as they approached the crystal, the blue light grew cold, and the room plunged into shadow. A figure stepped out from behind the pedestal, and the air grew thick with tension. It was Earnest, his eyes filled with a mix of desperation and regret. "I can't let you do this," he said, his voice strained. "The Time Keeper has promised me—"

"What?" Janet's voice was ice. "What could they possibly offer you that would make you betray us?" Earnest's eyes fell to the ground. "They promised to rewrite my past," he murmured. "To give me the life I was meant to have." He looked up, the desperation in his eyes raw. "The legend I was created to be." The revelation hit Eleanor like a punch to the gut. "You've been working with them?" she exclaimed, her voice filled with disbelief and anger. "I had to," Earnest said, his eyes pleading. "You don't know what it's like, to live in the shadows of your own story. To never achieve what you know you're capable of." His hand hovered over the Heart of Chronos, the crystal's pulse growing stronger. "But you're wrong," Eleanor said, her voice steady. "You are your own legend, Earnest. Your story isn't written yet."

"You don't understand," he insisted, the crystal's light casting a cold, blue hue over his features. "The Time Keeper showed me a version of my past where I didn't fail. Where I wasn't just a forgotten detective." Janet took a step closer, her voice low and measured. "And what of us?" she asked. "What of the world? The lives they're altering?" Earnest's grip on the Heart of Chronos tightened. "I never meant for it to go this far," he said, his voice thick with regret. "But I had to try." Pippa stepped forward, her eyes shimmering with understanding. "You want to change the pain," she said gently. "But you can't." Sir Bertrand's voice was firm. "We stand with you, Earnest, but not in this. Not if it means the unraveling of all we hold dear." For a moment, the detective looked torn, the weight of his decision etched into the lines of his face. Then, with a heavy sigh, he nodded. "I see that now," he murmured. "But I've gone too far. There's no turning back."

Eleanor took a deep breath, the scent of dust and ink filling her nostrils. "We're all just looking for our place in the story," she said, her eyes never leaving Earnest's. "But you're more than a character in a book. You're our friend." She extended her hand. "Please, give us the Heart of Chronos. Together, we can stop the Time Keeper." For a heartbeat, the room was silent. Then, slowly, Earnest reached out, his hand trembling as he placed the crystal into hers. The blue light grew dimmer, the books around them sighing as if in relief. "Thank you," she whispered, her voice filled with a mix of gratitude and sadness.

"I'm sorry," he murmured. "For everything." Janet stepped forward, her gaze softening. "We all make mistakes," she said. "But it's how we fix them that counts." Pippa offered him a small smile, her dagger now sheathed. "And you're not the only one who's ever felt like they're living in the shadows," she added. "But together, we can write our own legends." The detective nodded, the weight of his decision evident in his posture. "But how do we stop them?" he asked, his eyes searching theirs for answers.

Eleanor clutched the Heart of Chronos, its power thrumming through her veins. "We have to find the source of the Time Keeper's power," she said, her voice firm. "The place where they're anchored to our world. That's where we'll find them." The group looked around the chamber, the blue light from the crystal casting an eerie glow on the ancient tomes. "The library," Janet said, her voice grim. "They've been using the library as their gateway."

"But the library is vast," Pippa pointed out. "Where do we even begin?" The gold-foiled book in Janet's hand began to pulse, the pages flipping rapidly. "Here," she said, her finger stabbing at a page. "The library's foundation—it's where the original manuscripts are kept. That's where they'll be." The four of them looked at each other, determination etched on their faces. "To the basement," Sir Bertrand said, leading the way. They raced through the shifting corridors, dodging the phantoms of forgotten history that swirled around them. The air grew colder, the shelves more ancient, as they descended deeper into the library's bowels. The heartbeat of the Heart of Chronos grew louder, the pulse resonating through the very stones. "We're close," Eleanor murmured, her eyes on the book. The pages were now almost transparent, the blue ink pulsing in time with the crystal.

"The foundation," Janet panted. "We're almost there." The group exchanged grim nods, the gravity of the situation weighing heavily upon them. They burst into a cavernous room, the walls lined with ancient manuscripts, the scent of ancient parchment and mildew thick in the air. In the center, a swirling vortex of ink and light—the gateway to the Time Keeper's realm. "They're already here," Sir Bertrand murmured, his sword at the ready. "We must be swift and decisive." The Time Keeper emerged from the swirling mass, their eyes alight with the madness of power. "You've arrived just in time for the grand finale," they said with a chuckle, holding the gold-foiled book in their grasp. "I shall rewrite the very inception of this library, and with it, the concept of time itself. No more pesky custodians to thwart my plans!"

Eleanor's eyes narrowed. "You will not win," she said, her voice steady despite the fear that clawed at her heart. "We've come too far, learned too much." The Time Keeper's grin widened. "Ah, but knowledge is fleeting, my dear," they taunted. "Especially when it's erased from existence." Their hand hovered over the manuscripts, the quill poised to strike. "We won't let you," Janet snarled, her hand tightening around the Heart of Chronos. "You think you can stop me?" The Time Keeper's laughter was like shattering glass. Sir Bertrand stepped forward, his sword pointing at the swirling vortex. "We shall see," he said, his voice filled with the promise of battle. "Guard the Heart," Eleanor instructed, her eyes never leaving the Time Keeper. "I'll handle this." She strode towards the whirlwind of ink, her eyes on the gold-foiled book that contained the essence of their world. "You're just a librarian," the Time Keeper spat. "What can you possibly do?"

Chapter 12:

"I am the custodian of knowledge," Eleanor replied, her voice echoing through the chamber. "And I will not let you defile it." The air grew colder, and the pages of the books around them fluttered with the beginnings of a tempest. The Time Keeper raised their hand, and a blast of icy air shot towards her. She ducked, rolling to the side, and came up with the blue book held before her like a shield. "You dare challenge me?" the Time Keeper roared, their form becoming more and more insubstantial, as if made of the very pages of the books they sought to destroy. "We are the guardians of the narrative!" Janet called out, her voice strong.

"And we will not stand by as you tear it apart," Pippa added, her dagger flashing through the air. The Time Keeper's eyes flicked to each of them in turn, and for a moment, a flicker of doubt passed over their features. But then they laughed again, the sound grating and mad. "You're too late," they said. "The story has already begun to change." The walls of the library rippled around them, historical figures and events fading in and out like ghosts. The Heart of Chronos grew brighter in Eleanor's hand, its light casting strange shadows on the manuscripts that surrounded them.

"Now, watch as I rewrite your very beginnings!" The Time Keeper plunged the quill into the gold-foiled book, and the ink spilled out, spreading like a stain over the manuscripts. The pages writhed and shrank, the stories they contained screaming in silent agony. "No!" Eleanor shouted, and with all her strength, she flung the Heart of Chronos into the vortex. The crystal exploded in a burst of blue light, and the swirling ink froze, the quill hovering in midair. "You can't do this," she panted, her eyes locked on the Time Keeper's fading form. The room trembled as the very fabric of reality stretched and warped. The Time Keeper's laughter grew distant, the pages of the books around them fluttering with the echoes of a thousand untold futures.

"We must hold the line," Sir Bertrand called, his sword slashing through the air to deflect a tendril of ink that reached for Pippa. She danced back, her eyes focused on the enemy. "We stand as the guardians of the story," Janet said, her voice ringing through the chaos. Earnest nodded, his detective instincts honed sharp. "And we will not let it be rewritten!" The Time Keeper's eyes flashed with rage at the interruption. "Fools," they hissed, the quill in their hand crackling with energy. "You cannot stop what is written!" The air grew thick with the scent of ozone as the ritual's power grew, the pages of the library's foundation manuscripts writhing in protest.

"The Heart!" Janet shouted, pointing to the crystal that lay at the center of the vortex, its light flickering. "It's weakening them!" Eleanor saw her chance and lunged, the blue book a beacon in her hand. The Time Keeper's form grew less solid, the pages of their being threatening to disintegrate into the maelstrom of time. "Give me the book!" she demanded. The Time Keeper's laughter was a cacophony of history's whispers. "You think you can wield it?"

THE PAGES OF TIME

"We're the guardians of the world's story," Eleanor said, her voice steady despite the chaos around her. "And we won't let you take that away from us." With a roar, Sir Bertrand charged, his sword slicing through the air as if it were paper. The Time Keeper stumbled, their grip on the gold-foiled book loosening. Pippa took advantage of the distraction, darting forward to grab the book. The moment she touched it, the pages fluttered open to reveal the prophecy of their confrontation. "The Time Keeper's fall," she read aloud, her voice resonating with power.

The room grew still, the ink tendrils retreating. The Time Keeper's form flickered, their power waning. "You're too late," they snarled. "The narrative has already been altered." Eleanor stepped closer, her eyes on the book. "But it hasn't been finished," she said softly. "Not yet." With a deep breath, she placed her hand on the gold-foiled cover. The pages grew warm, the words shifting beneath her fingertips. "What are you doing?" Janet demanded, fear etching her features. "I'm rewriting the ending," Eleanor murmured. "The only way to stop them is to become what they fear most."

"No!" Janet's voice was a cry. "You can't sacrifice yourself!" But Eleanor's gaze was firm, her eyes filled with a quiet resolve. "This isn't just about us," she said. "It's about Dunsford, the world, It's about the stories we all share." The Time Keeper's eyes grew wide, their laughter dying in their throat. "You would doom yourself?" They spat the words, their form becoming less stable. "If it means saving the narrative," Eleanor said, "then yes." With a surge of power, she tore the prophecy from the pages, the ink searing into her hand like a brand. The air shimmered around her as the blue book in her other hand grew heavier.

"Eleanor, no!" Pippa reached for her, but Sir Bertrand held her back. "This is her path," he murmured. "We must trust her." Eleanor stepped into the vortex, the pages of the library's foundation manuscripts swirling around her like a tornado. The Time Keeper's form flickered, their eyes filled with a desperate hunger. "You cannot do this!" they shrieked, but their voice was drowned out by the roar of time itself. "You are not the narrator!" Eleanor shouted back. "You are but a scribe!" The gold-foiled book grew hot in her grasp, the prophecy pulsing in time with the beating of her heart. The blue light of the Heart of Chronos grew brighter, the crystal's power melding with hers. "I am the Gaurdian!" she screamed, the words echoing through the library. "And I will not let you destroy our story!" With a final surge of strength, she flung the prophecy into the Time Keeper's chest. The figure staggered back, the pages of their being fluttering away like leaves on the wind.

Chapter 13:

The room grew silent as the blue light grew blinding, enveloping everything. The air grew thick with the scent of ancient ink and the whispers of countless voices from the pages of history. The Time Keeper's eyes went wide with understanding, then despair as the reality of their fate sank in. "You... you can't," they murmured, their voice fading. "But I must," Eleanor said, her own voice now distant, as if she were speaking through a veil. The light grew so bright she could barely see her friends, their forms fading with each passing moment.

"Eleanor, no!" Janet's cry was filled with anguish, but she was powerless to stop her. The blue light washed over the group, the pages of the manuscripts fluttering around them, each one a testament to the lives that could be erased. "Remember, the books," Eleanor whispered, her voice growing fainter. "Guard them with your lives." And with that, she disappeared into the light.

For a moment, there was only silence. Then, the air grew thick with the scent of burnt parchment, and the light began to dim. The Time Keeper's form grew solid again, their eyes wide with shock and anger. "You think you've won?" they hissed, their fists clenching. "You've doomed us all!" But as they spoke, the pages of the manuscripts grew still, the blue light receding into the Heart of Chronos. The library's foundation stabilized, the air growing warm with the promise of restored order.

"Eleanor," Janet whispered, her eyes searching the fading light for any sign of their friend. "What have you done?" The blue book lay open on the floor, the pages now blank. "I've done what had to be done," came Eleanor's voice, now distant and ethereal. "The story continues without me." The Time Keeper staggered, their power waning. "You... you can't," they whispered, their form flickering like a candle in a storm. "I am the guardian," Eleanor said, her voice echoing through the chamber. "And I will not let you rewrite the truth." With a final burst of power, she pushed the Time Keeper into the vortex, the pages of the library's history swirling around them, erasing them from existence.

The room grew still, the air thick with the scent of burnt parchment. Janet, Sir Bertrand, Pippa, and Earnest stared in disbelief at the spot where Eleanor had stood, their hearts heavy with grief. "What now?" Earnest asked, his voice cracking. "Now," Janet said, her eyes hardening, "we honor her sacrifice." The Heart of Chronos grew dimmer, the blue light fading from its core. "We must ensure that the library returns to its rightful state," Sir Bertrand murmured. The gold-foiled book lay open on the floor, its pages now as white and unblemished as freshly fallen snow. Janet picked it up with trembling hands, her eyes scanning the empty pages. "We have to fix this," she murmured. "We can't let her sacrifice be in vain." Pippa nodded, her grip tight on her dagger. "We will," she said firmly. "But how?"

Sir Bertrand stepped forward, the weight of his centuries-long guardianship heavy on his shoulders. "We must find a way to restore the balance," he said, his voice steady. "The

THE PAGES OF TIME 51

library is the nexus of all time and knowledge. We must ensure it remains untouched by the Time Keeper's taint." His gaze fell on the Heart of Chronos, now pulsating gently in Janet's hand. "The power lies within this crystal," he mused. "We must harness it wisely." Pippa looked around the chamber, her eyes shining with determination. "We need to return to the surface, gather the townsfolk, and prepare for whatever comes next," she said. "The Time Keeper's influence may still be felt." Janet nodded, her eyes never leaving the book. "We will rebuild the narrative," she said, her voice filled with resolve. "We'll make sure the story goes on, as it should."

Sir Bertrand took a step towards the exit, his sword still drawn. "We must act swiftly," he said. "The fabric of time is delicate. The longer we wait, the more damage could be done." As they moved through the library, the books began to right themselves, the air warming as if a great burden had been lifted. The town of Dunsford slowly materialized outside the windows, the clock tower standing tall once again. The group exchanged looks, the weight of their victory tempered by the cost.

"Eleanor," Janet whispered, clutching the gold-foiled book to her chest. "We've lost her." The blue light of the Heart of Chronos grew brighter, the crystal pulsing with power. "We've lost a friend," Sir Bertrand said, his eyes sad. "But we've gained a legend." Pippa nodded, her hand resting on Janet's shoulder. "And we will ensure she's never forgotten." Earnest looked around the chamber, his gaze lingering on the spot where Eleanor had vanished. "We must honor her," he said firmly. "We must protect the library, the books, and the knowledge she loved so much."

Together, they approached the crystal pedestal, the Heart of Chronos still beating with a faint light. Janet took the book and placed it upon the pedestal. The light grew stronger, the pages fluttering to life. "The narrative has been restored," she murmured. "But the cost..." Her voice trailed off as she looked at the others. "We must carry on her legacy," Sir Bertrand said, his eyes steely. "We will be the guardians of the library." The words hung in the air, a solemn vow that bound them together.

"Eleanor would want us to keep the library safe," Pippa said, her voice thick with unshed tears. "And we will. We'll make sure that no one else tries to alter the Story." Janet nodded, her grip on the Heart of Chronos tight. "We'll protect the knowledge within these walls," she vowed. "We'll be the Guardians of time." The Heart of Chronos pulsed in response, the light growing brighter, and the books around them settled into their rightful places. "But what of the prophecy?" Earnest asked, his eyes on the gold-foiled book. "What becomes of us now?" The pages of the book fluttered, and Janet read aloud. "The guardians shall rise, and the Time Keeper fall. The library will endure, though the price be great." She looked up, her expression grim. "It's over," she murmured. "Eleanor was the price."

Sir Bertrand sheathed his sword, his gaze on the Heart of Chronos. "We must ensure that no one else ever pays such a cost," he said. "The library is safe, but our work has only just begun." Pippa nodded, her eyes on the swirling blue light. "We will train, learn from the books, and be ready for whatever the future holds." The words hung in the air, a promise to the absent Eleanor.

Chapter 14:

Months passed, and the library once again became a sanctuary of quiet solitude. The townsfolk returned to their mundane routines, the whispers of the extraordinary fading like the ink on the pages of forgotten books. Yet, beneath the veneer of normalcy, the guardians remained vigilant. They had become a part of the library's fabric, its protectors unseen. "Remember," Janet would say to them often, her eyes on the spot where Eleanor had vanished, "we are the keepers of the Story now."

"IT'S STRANGE," PIPPA mused one evening, her eyes on the swirling patterns of the Heart of Chronos. "We've defeated the Time Keeper, restored the narrative... yet the whispers persist." Sir Bertrand nodded gravely. "Their influence lingers," he said. "But we will not let it take hold again." They had turned the hidden chamber into a sanctum, a place where they studied the ancient texts and honed their skills, preparing for any new threats that might arise.

"We owe it to Eleanor," Janet said, her voice thick with emotion. "To keep the library safe, and the story intact." She glanced at the spot where the blue book had once been, now a simple stone pedestal. It had been months since the battle, and the gold-foiled book remained open on the shelf, a silent sentinel to the truth of their adventure. "Aye," Sir Bertrand agreed, his hand on the hilt of his sword. "We are the guardians now." The weight of his words settled in the room, a solemn vow that seemed to echo off the ancient stones. Earnest nodded, his eyes reflecting the candlelight. "We'll make her proud."

"We must be vigilant," Janet warned. "The Time Keeper might have been defeated, but their kind do not easily relinquish power." Pippa nodded solemnly, her eyes scanning the shelves as if expecting the books to whisper warnings. Sir Bertrand agreed. "We've seen the power of narratives, the way they can shape reality. We cannot rest on our laurels." He glanced at the gold-foiled book, its pages now as white and unblemished as the day it had been created. "The story continues, and so must we." The group gathered around the stone pedestal where the Heart of Chronos now rested, a constant reminder of their duty. "We're not just guardians of the library," Pippa said, her gaze flickering to the blue book's empty spot. "We're guardians of time itself." Earnest nodded, his expression determined. "And we'll train new custodians, pass on what we've learned." Janet nodded, her eyes misty. "In doing so, we keep Eleanor's legacy alive." They each placed a hand upon the cool stone, feeling the faint pulse of the crystal beneath their fingertips.

"We'll protect the books," Pippa vowed, her voice echoing through the chamber. "The stories within them are the threads that weave the fabric of existence." Sir Bertrand nodded gravely. "And we'll continue to share those stories with the children of Dunsford," he said. "To inspire them as Eleanor did." Janet's eyes lit up with a spark of hope. "Yes," she said, "we'll ensure the next generation understands the power of knowledge and the importance of guardianship."

The guardians stood in silence for a moment, the weight of their responsibility settling upon them. Then, as if on cue, the Heart of Chronos pulsed with a gentle light, the pages of the gold-foiled book fluttered, and the room was filled with whispers of long-forgotten tales. It was a sign, a reminder that the library was more than just a collection of dusty tomes. It was a living, breathing entity that required their care. "The story goes on," Janet murmured, her hand resting on the book. "And so do we."

Days turned into weeks, and the guardians threw themselves into their new roles. They patrolled the library's shadowy corners, ensuring that no more anomalies would threaten the town. They cataloged the books with renewed purpose, each title a thread in the tapestry of time they had sworn to protect. And in the quiet moments, when the last patron had left and the candles burned low, Janet would pull out one of the ancient tomes and read aloud, the words a tribute to their absent friend.

One evening, as she thumbed through the pages of a dusty volume on historical myths, Janet's eyes fell upon a piece of parchment, folded and tucked neatly between the brittle pages. She gasped as she recognized the handwriting. "Eleanor Marks," she whispered, her heart racing as she unfolded the note. It read:

"My dear Janet, Sir Bertrand, Pippa, and Earnest," Janet read aloud, her voice trembling with hope. "If you are reading this, it means my plan has succeeded, and you are the guardians of the library now." The room grew silent, the candles flickering as if in response to the revelation. "What does it mean?" Pippa breathed, her hand over her mouth. "It means," Janet said, her eyes scanning the note, "that she knew the price she might pay." Sir Bertrand took the parchment, his brow furrowed. "The language is cryptic, but it seems she had foreseen this outcome." Earnest leaned in, his eyes widening as Janet continued. "Her sacrifice was not in vain. The narrative lives on, and within it, so does she."

The note spoke of an unexplored chapter in the library's history, a hidden part of the story that only the most devoted custodian could uncover. It hinted at the possibility of restoring Eleanor, of bringing her back to the library she had so fiercely protected. "But how?" Pippa asked, her voice hushed. "The book is blank, the prophecy erased." Janet folded the note, her expression determined. "We'll find a way," she said, her eyes on the swirling light of the Heart of Chronos. "We have the power of the library behind us, and the knowledge of the guardians before us."

Sir Bertrand nodded slowly, his gaze on Janet. "We must study the ancient texts," he said. "Perhaps there is a spell, an incantation that can reverse the flow of time, bring her back to us." Pippa's eyes widened with hope. "Could it be true?" she whispered. "Could we save her?" Janet took a deep breath. "We have to try," she said firmly. "For Dunsford, for the library, and for Eleanor."

Earnest spoke up, his voice tentative. "But if we meddle with time," he said, "what are the consequences? Could we make things worse?" Pippa placed a hand on his arm. "We can't live in fear of what might happen," she said. "Eleanor showed us that. We have to have faith in our ability to set things right." Janet nodded. "We'll be careful," she promised. "We'll find a way that doesn't risk the narrative we've worked so hard to preserve."

THE PAGES OF TIME

They huddled around the Heart of Chronos, the crystal's gentle light casting blue shadows on their faces. "We'll start with the prophecy," Janet decided. "If we can understand how she was taken from us, perhaps we can find a way to bring her back." They pored over the gold-foiled book, each page a silent testament to their shared history. "Here," Sir Bertrand said, pointing to a faint line of text that hadn't been there before. "It speaks of the guardian who gave themselves to the narrative." Janet leaned closer, her eyes widening. "It says," she read, "that the essence of the one who wields the blue book may not be lost, but rather dispersed through the very fabric of time and story."

"What does that mean?" Pippa asked, her voice filled with hope. "Could she be... alive?" "Possibly," Janet murmured, her eyes scanning the page. "But scattered, lost in the pages of countless narratives." They looked at each other, the implication of their discovery sinking in. "We must find a way to reach her," Pippa said, her grip on the book tightening. "To pull her back from the stories she's become a part of."

Sir Bertrand stroked his chin thoughtfully. "The blue book," he mused. "It's the key to her essence. We must use it to navigate the narrative threads, to locate where she might be hidden." Janet nodded, a spark of hope igniting in her eyes. "We'll need to be careful," she said. "The blue book is powerful, and the narratives it contains can be... volatile, but perhaps Eleanor's sacrifice isn't as final as we feared and somewhere, somewhen she still might exist."

Don't miss out!

Visit the website below and you can sign up to receive emails whenever Art Vulcan publishes a new book. There's no charge and no obligation.

https://books2read.com/r/B-A-MJTMC-NKLDF

BOOKS 2 READ

Connecting independent readers to independent writers.